THE REVOLT

On 2 September 1939, in the darkness of wartime Paris, two lovers part tenderly at Le Bourget Airport. Einar, a Swede, feels compelled to return to his neutral country. He leaves behind Olga, a young Russian émigrée. They are very much in love and exchange promises, pledging each to the other. It is seven years before they meet again.

Throughout the war and beyond, questions of hope and despair lie behind everything Olga does. 'Is he alive? Will I ever see him again?' A trip to Stockholm provides the answers. Einar is now married to the voluptuous Emma, whose cherubic face masks a devious nature. Then, against all expectation, there is a chance for Olga to fulfil her dreams. But the price is high.

Nina Berberova writes as others engrave on brass: her style is fine, neat and precise. Her spare and rich prose expresses emotion with an intensity and sincerity that makes this superb novella a masterpiece.

Nina Berberova

---❖---

THE REVOLT

Translated from the Russian by
Marian Schwartz

COLLINS
8 Grafton Street, London W1
1989

William Collins Sons & Co. Ltd
London · Glasgow · Sydney · Auckland
Toronto · Johannesburg

BRITISH LIBRARY CATALOGUING IN PUBLICATION DATA

Berberova, Nina, *1901–*
The revolt
I. Title
891.73'44 [F]

ISBN 0–00–223437–8

First published in Great Britain in 1989

Typeset in Linotron Pilgrim at The Spartan Press Ltd,
Lymington, Hants
Printed and bound in Great Britain by
Hartnolls Ltd, Bodmin, Cornwall

THE REVOLT

ONE

———◇———

IN EVERYONE'S LIFE there are moments when unexpec-
tedly, for no apparent reason, a door that has been shut
suddenly cracks open, a trellised window, only just
lowered, goes up, a sharp, seemingly final 'no' becomes
a 'perhaps', and in that second the world around us is
transformed and we ourselves are filled, transfused,
with hopes. A postponement is granted to something
inevitable, final; the decision of the judge, the doctor,
the consul, is set aside. A voice informs us that all is
not yet lost. And on trembling legs, with tears of
gratitude, we pass on to the next station, where we are
asked to 'wait a moment' before we are plunged into
the abyss.

That's how it was for me that evening as I stood next
to Einar in the line of departing passengers being bused
to Le Bourget for the flight to Stockholm. He was
leaving, I was staying. In the crowd, at that dark Paris
intersection (it was 2 September 1939), at nine o'clock
in the evening, were only those leaving – the others
seeing someone off had all been told to remain in the

waiting-room, which had already been hung with blackout blinds. In there had been the farewells, embraces, even tears, and, naturally, the unclutching of children's hands from someone's sleeves and pockets. I walked out with Einar, almost automatically, through the revolving door. In one arm he carried a fat briefcase, in the other a leather travel case. His coat was draped over his right arm. My hand held his fingers under that coat and touched the leather case's cold lock. Einar kept glancing over at me. In the semi-darkness his face seemed strange, weary, distraught; the firm lines of his cheekbones and chin, which I had so loved, were lost. There was disquiet in his eyes and his mouth gaped. He's ugly, I thought, on the verge of tears and unable to tell him: 'I didn't know you were so ugly.' Tickets and papers in hand, the passengers were boarding the bus. Einar switched his coat to his left arm, and I withdrew mine, to take his case. He held out his papers.

'And you?' I couldn't talk, I was afraid of my own voice; one good look at me and anyone could tell that I wasn't flying to Stockholm.

'Would you like to ride to Le Bourget?' a uniformed worker asked me.

'I . . .'

'Climb in. Don't hold up the others.'

Even now I can't believe those words. Could something like that actually have happened? And why specifically to me? I hadn't asked for anything, and anyway, would it ever really occur to anyone to ask an official for anything of the kind? I scrambled up the steps, and in silence we (Einar ahead, me behind) walked back to the last seats and sat down. He put his arm around me and I leaned up against his shoulder, his chest, so broad and calm, where Einar's heart was beating, as I had heard it all those last sleepless nights.

Slowly the bus filled. Through the window you could see the porters scurrying to load the baggage on to the roof. Over our heads we could hear noisy footsteps; someone came running out of the dark to one of the windows and asked something, and a voice from the bus answered him in Swedish. The driver, wearing a white jacket, walked down the aisle and counted on his fingers those seated, skipping me. The engine was started up, the door shut. A few people ran out of the waiting-room and waved handkerchiefs, and gradually we got underway. I pressed even closer to Einar.

'You're ugly right now,' I finally got out, and suddenly I felt like laughing. He probably thought I was crying, because he ran his finger over my eyelids. I grabbed his hand and pressed his palm to my lips. Those minutes were my gift! A stay had been granted! It was all of one hour, but in those moments that seemed like a great deal.

Dark Paris, dead Paris, but that night not black, rather a kind of dark green. The entire city, and the sky up above, and the river, and the inside of the bus – everything was dark green, bottle green: our faces, and the faces of the other passengers, and the Grand Palais, which we rumbled past, were all the same colour. The thick dark window pane imprisoned us, him and me, and the city as well. Those streets, which we both knew so well and which now were racing by, belonged to the same strange, dark green world as Einar and me; and we realized that he and I still had a lot that we hadn't managed to discuss in the rush of the last days, especially that very last day. We had left so much unsaid: about him and me and also about the outside world, having to do with the war and the future – again both the world's and ours – and in general it was as if we had never begun anything. It seemed to me that he and I had never had a past, and there was nothing to say about the future – a spectre ahead, a spectre behind, we were both spectres, and all around us was spectral, and of it all the only thing real was that force tearing us asunder: right now you're here, with me, right now we're together, but in an hour you won't be here; you're alone, I'm alone, and there's nothing whatsoever to keep us together other than an idea – yours about me and mine about you.

'You and Paris . . .' Einar was saying, but precisely what he was saying I wasn't following. 'Promise me, Olga . . .' What on earth? He knew I would promise him whatever he asked. Maybe I was the one who should have said: 'Promise me.' But there's still time. Later.

'Paris, you, all that went on . . .' and again he was saying something my brain couldn't take in, knowing full well that I really ought to make the effort, that there would be no such occasion tomorrow, nor the day after tomorrow, maybe not next year either. Beyond that I could not begin to imagine. The thick glass, dark green bottle into which I had fallen (and from which he was about to emerge) was not going to break for a long time; autumn and winter days, black wartime nights, would come when I would be alone.

'. . . and in constant danger,' Einar was saying, as if, as usual, reading my thoughts, 'with a constant shortage of necessities. Promise me, Olga . . .'

And I, still holding his hand to my lips, whispered: 'But of course.'

I remember earlier, many years before, I could take a detached look at Paris, aloof, cool, and think: What a lot of history here! or: What a lot of beauty here! or even: What a lot of nature here! (sky, birds, flowers). Or: What a lot of monuments and books, graves and marble plaques – 'So and so lived here.' But now I watched the embankment trees swimming past and thought: What a lot of suffering here, past, present, and future, not just suffering in general but our Russian suffering, and now my own! Turgenev's sufferings in his home on the rue de Douai, and Dostoevsky's in his hotel on the Boulevard Saint-Michel. And the sufferings of the long forgotten author of those lines about the river having such a pronounced bend, who committed suicide here, even before the 'other' war (I saw his grave once; the stone still stands, but wild rose bushes have wholly enlaced it). And the suffering of a certain artist stranded in Europe's capitals (Does anyone still remember his name?) who came here and stayed here and said: 'Curse though I may, I'm staying' – until he swallowed some powders and, as can happen, was not saved. And now my own sufferings, great and small, as we approach the Opera.

'We're going uphill, do you feel it?' said Einar. 'I never noticed it, and I know this section so well!'

Everything was dead. Only last evening everything here had been arumble, lit up, and the dark green gloom had been a novelty for these streets, and buildings, and sky, and pavement, which for me for so many years had been the colour of lilac and hollyhocks.

'Everything's different today,' he said again, very very quietly. 'I look at you and I look out the window and I can't believe, I simply can't believe that there could ever come an end to all this.'

He looked into my eyes and, smiling, asked, 'What poem is there about that?'

He was making fun of me. He always said that in Russian there was invariably a poem for each and every life event.

'I already have one,' I said. 'Ever since we got going. But I won't tell it to you.'

'Yes, you will!'

'It was when I was telling you I never knew you were so ugly.'

We both became quiet. The Gare du Nord, dark green in the dark green of the boulevard, was left behind.

'When you come to Stockholm . . .' That was one of the fairy-tales he sometimes told me. Another was: When you and I go to Brazil . . . And a third: When we return to Russia . . . He didn't know Russian, had never been in Russia, was a Swede born and bred, but his father in his youth had spent some time in Petersburg, spoke Russian, and now, widowed, lived in his home with a Russian nursemaid, who, in some way I didn't quite understand, had become one of the family, complete with icons and samovar. In a photograph I knew well, there he sat, paralysed, in an armchair, gaunt, tall, resembling no one so much as King Gustav, and next to him, half a step back, wearing a kerchief and embroidered apron, stood this nursemaid, heavy of body but with a wrinkled little face, leaning up against a door-jamb, her chin resting in her palm.

'When you come to Stockholm,' said Einar, 'and go for a walk in the royal park, you'll see someone in one of the palace windows, the upper left, seeming to conduct with one arm – that's our king embroidering cross-stitch.'

'And when we go to Brazil?'

'When we go to Brazil we'll have to find out whether the diamond mines my mother's father owned still exist. At one time they brought in a lot of money, later they stopped, and now evidently the weeds have taken over. No one's heard a word about them for the longest time.'

'Are you sure it's in Brazil and not Rhodesia?'

'That's what my brother told me.'

'And when we return to Russia?'

'We must go to Russia for nanny's sake. She's from Kurgany, a village in the *volost* of Lukino in the district of Vesyegonsk. We have to take her there. She gets very homesick for it sometimes.'

'There are no more *volosts*.'

'District of Vesyegonsk, province of Tver.'

'Or districts either. You tell her.'

'So what are there?'

'Regions, republics.'

'All right, I'll tell her.'

The broad straight road taking us out of the city raced under our wheels, and so did time, head on and past.

North-east. For some reason I've long been of the belief that north-east is an unlucky, dreadful, sinister direction. It's time I tracked down where I ever got this idea. An airplane flies to the north-east and never returns. There is never any news from the north-east. Enemies come from the north-east. Someone left for the north-east and was never seen again. Enough! Stop my thought for me, please; I can't do it myself. Let's talk of Brazil, of Rhodesia. Or let's talk of the war.

'It began this morning.'

'Was it really only this morning? It feels like it's been going on forever.'

His two hands, my two, and all four holding on tightly to each other. That still won't help. Right now, as we roll along in this bus, yes, but later – no. Another twenty minutes to go, eighteen maybe.

A crowd of recruits is marching in the utter darkness and we overtake them, lurching to one side with such force that my whole body leans into Einar and once again we look at one another.

'You won't forget me?' he asks all of a sudden.

'An unworthy question, unworthy of you.'

'Promise?'

'Promise. What else is there to promise?'

'Anything you want. I'll take whatever you've got.'

He held me close. We didn't talk after that. I wasn't allowed off the bus. I pressed my face to the pane, the way they used to write in novels: 'The countess reclined on her chaise, and the count pressed his burning brow to the cold window . . .'

Dark blue lamps, like enormous night-lights, burned in the dark green night. Was this not an underwater kingdom? Had we not drowned? Einar was waving at me, having set his case on the ground. He was the last one, all the others having already passed through the wide gates.

'Einar!' I ran to the exit in order to jump down, run to those gates, and cry out: 'Einar! Farewell! Live happily on firm ground. We're drowning, Einar, we're going to drown, and if we do survive we won't be the same as we were anyway . . .'

But the bus door had been locked from without, they were acting as if I weren't inside, and there was nobody else around. I sat down on the first seat and looked through the window again: no one, nothing. Until the driver came in, the same one who had counted the passengers on his fingers and skipped me. He didn't say anything, started the motor, turned cautiously, made a U-turn, and we drove back, calmly, steadily. I opened the window, the wind whistled through my hair. In the distance the city, dark green with a hint of olive, was getting closer and closer. With a long shudder in my breast the tears spurted from my eyes, but I stopped them. It was as if I had stopped altogether and was looking back at everything that had happened to me. But reality in the past and present is all twisted and smashed: a painting both incomplete and overdone. The wind is whistling through my hair and already here is that watchtower we passed before, and here is that intersection. And soon those same streets, those same buildings will go by; soon this entire fantasy trip (which no one will believe, which I myself don't believe) will end. The window will close, the door will slam shut, pinching someone's living flesh, and life will go on, like a dark green river.

And in the darkness, the crowd of recruits is still marching, marching.

TWO

◆

SEVEN LONG YEARS of separation. Einar was right: we
Russians have a poem for each and every life event.
From that evening when I came home to Dmitrii
Georgievich's vast, silent apartment, where I lived as
his niece-cum-secretary-cum-boarder, up to the day I
saw Einar again, seven years passed.

Returning home, I passed soundlessly through the
rooms and knocked at Dmitrii Georgievich's study. He
was sitting under a lamp, his legs wrapped in a plaid,
wearing his old camel-hair cardigan and a little cap.
He was seventy-nine years old then. He doesn't look
like Gustav of Sweden, he looks like a Chinese
emperor, I thought. He said he had had his supper and
had worked and was now reading and needed nothing,
so I went to my room and lay down without undressing
– and lay there like that till morning, sleepless,
powerless, just thinking over and over how it all had
been, how it all would be.

Having married my mother's sister, Dmitrii Georgievich – still long before my birth – forced his wife's

entire family to become serious, and by the time I came into the world idleness had come to be considered the world's greatest sin. If Dmitrii Georgievich was writing books, attending conferences, giving lectures, and maintaining direct contact with many of the world's academies, then all of us were equally expected to do something useful. My first memory: I've barely turned three, I'm standing in the middle of the room feeling tremendous, crushing guilt, and my mother is asking me gravely: 'What are you busy with?'

'Nothing.'

'Go, get busy. How can you waste time?'

Now, of all those active, strong, healthy, anti-time wasting people, all that remained were the two of us – I and the Chinese emperor, meek, quiet, taciturn, ever content, sometimes sad, wearing two pairs of glasses on his nose, with his plaid, his little cap, buttressed all around with books, green-shaded lamps; surrounded by papers, letters, translations of his own and others' papers. Around him were his boxes of used stamps, unused stamps, pencil ends, pins and paper-clips; around him lay scatter cushions 'from the time of the conquest of the Crimea' (I don't remember which) and notebooks with crimson bookmarks, one of them embroidered in old-fashioned script: 'Take a book but put it back.'

During the first year of the war, before the fall of Paris, letters came from Einar, and he even wrote that he might come in the spring on business, 'And then you'll see how fine everything will be.' But he didn't. In the spring things began to happen: more than ever, Dmitrii Georgievich, draped with his plaid, sat in his armchair and read, spoke softly and only the bare minimum. More and more often he dozed or sat, his eyes shut, his small dry hands – the fingers of which, with their carefully manicured nails, were bent with rheumatism – resting on his knees, and this asymmetry of the bones in his hands was very characteristic of him.

On the day of Paris's capture, while the German army was traversing it from north-east to south-west, life in our apartment went on – as it did, by the way, in many other parts of the city: several cinemas stayed open, and the Metro didn't stop for a minute. It was strange, later, to picture that day: an enemy army taking the capital while underground the trains are speeding; in the Bibliothèque Nationale someone is sitting over some engravings; and we, Dmitrii Georgievich and I, are lunching on fried eggs, salad, and cheese, while the teary-eyed maid walks from the kitchen to the dining-room and back; both of us silent, but perhaps no more so than we had been yesterday or the day before. And the Chinese emperor, putting his fork down, goes over to the window and looks out at the street, at the dense trees of the Boulevard de Courcelles, under one of which a German soldier has stopped to answer nature's call.

Up until then I had worked at a newspaper, but now I had nothing but time on my hands for days on end. I didn't know what to do with myself until we let the

maid go. Then the house came to occupy my day.
Fearing a vacuum, I would either do laundry, or paint
the foyer, or copy something for Dmitrii Georgievich –
anything not to sit idle. Sometimes guests came: two
old ladies, one-time admirers, probably, of Dmitrii
Georgievich; his distant relative Elena Vikentievna,
who worked so hard in a millinery workshop. She
called Dmitrii Georgievich 'Nineteenth Century.'

'Is our Nineteenth Century well?'

'How are you getting along here with Nineteenth
Century?'

'Nineteenth Century is asleep,' I sometimes said,
and she would go, leaving a cake.

Four years – four visits. The first: a general ac-
companied by a young adjutant who came to 'pay his
respects to the great man' and to ask whether he might
be of any assistance. As was his wont, Dmitrii
Georgievich mostly kept quiet. I stood outside the door
and eavesdropped. The general offered to order necessary books, to send a box of food, recommended a
better foot-warmer. When he left, bowing respectfully
and asking for an autograph, I wondered at the silence
that had descended on the apartment. Dmitrii
Georgievich lay in his room, turned toward the wall. I
set about cleaning the silver – just the task I needed.
Outside the kitchen window airplanes flew in a tri-
angle, like geese.

'I'm going to turn into a real moron if I keep on this
way,' I told myself. 'Maybe I should reread some good
books?' To read new books did not occur to me at the

time. 'Say, *Paradise Regained* or *The History of the Russian State* or *Gulliver's Travels*?'

The second visit was during the second year. In the morning, at about eleven o'clock, there was a long, somehow cheerful ring, as if someone had finally caught up with us. I had never seen Dr Wengland before. For forty years, whenever Dmitrii Georgievich was in Berlin, he had stayed with Dr Wengland. Dr Wengland was a name I'd known since childhood. I remembered from the stories that during the 'other' war Dr Wengland, by means of some subtle ruse, had got word of himself to Dmitrii Georgievich in a roundabout way through Denmark. Dr Wengland was an inextricable part of life for all of us. The last time they had seen one another had been at some conference in Heidelberg, ten years or so before ('during the era of electrical prospecting for oil reserves,' as Dmitrii Georgievich's Swedish publisher, Olners, would have put it). Old, huge, jubilant, Dr Wengland burrowed through the rooms and embraced Dmitrii Georgievich and, wiping away the tears running from his eyes and sniffling loudly, went into his study. The doors were closed and it got quiet. I went to my room and slowly began wiping first the mirror of my dressing-table, then the windows from the inside, and when that too was done, crawled out and washed both windows, trying not to look down. And the whole time a wholly logical thought worried me: why not go ahead and look down (with all the consequences)? Why, standing on the sixth-floor ledge, be afraid of vertigo?

That day I ate my dinner alone. Dr Wengland left, and Dmitrii Georgievich sat down in the living-room by the fireplace, which was never laid and from which came a draft; the living-room that no one ever used. Dmitrii Georgievich gazed into the fireplace, his back turned to everything else, as if a fire danced there. From that day on he suddenly lost interest in his papers and books, and several times I caught him in front of the bookcase in the foyer which held everything brought from Russia at the start of the century. Those books had stood there untouched for a long time.

The third visit was quite brief: two tall, slender Adonises, badges on their sleeves, pins on their chests, and iron wings on their caps, swept through the apartment in a quick, rather cursory search, scarcely glanced into my room, confiscated two files of Dmitrii Georgievich's letters from various academic friends, and pushed him aside (he came up to their chests) when he tried to defend the centre drawer of his desk, which they yanked out and let dangle. Quickly rifling through a box of peppermint pastilles, a box of old erasers, and even a box of steel nibs of every possible description, they thanked him, apologized hastily, explaining that they were searching for weapons, and left. That evening I noticed that Dmitrii Georgievich was quite depressed, and I sat up with him until eleven, turned down his bed, spread his plaid. When he came back from the bathroom I saw that he, always so fastidious, had failed to wrap his bathrobe properly; his nightshirt stopped at his knees and his skinny yellow legs, veiny and lumpy, stuck out from underneath. I looked away. Paying me no heed he got in under the covers, dropped his dentures into a glass of water, and turned off the light. I tiptoed out.

Laundry was now out of the question – there was a shortage of soap. Likewise painting the walls: paint was too expensive. All our money went for food. I had nothing to sew, and anyway, there wasn't any thread. When I did have to sew on a button or mend a hole I pulled the thread out of the old one, taking care not to break it. I had nothing to do, nowhere to go. We had electric lights in the evening; at night they were turned off, and we lived in total darkness. Once in a while I lit a candle, read a half a page of *The History of the Pugachev Rebellion*, and set the book aside.

In March 1944 came the fourth and final visit. It happened at seven o'clock in the morning. I jumped up, awakened by insistent ringing. It was the French police – two in plain clothes and two, in uniform, of the kind that usually stand on corners directing traffic or give directions to passersby. The ones in uniform were as ordinary, fresh-faced, and broad-shouldered as could be, but I had never seen them in an apartment before, just as I had never seen a horse or a sheep in an apartment; they pertained to streets and roads, but in no way to rooms. They asked me to wake up Dmitrii Georgievich, waited for him to dress, and were even courteous enough to ask him to bring along a blanket. They insisted on carrying his suitcase, which I had packed with medications, jerseys, and socks. He had suddenly become a perfect dwarf, all hunched over. He tucked his cap into a pocket, put on the hat I gave him, and cautiously kissed first my cheek, then my hand, and I too kissed first his beard, then his hand, the police keeping their eyes on the ceiling all the while.

A few minutes later (I was still in the foyer, having no idea where to go now) the bell rang again. I remember being utterly unable to turn the lock; not only my hands but my entire self was trembling. Finally I did it.

'The professor wants to know whether you packed the strophanthus,' asked one of those in uniform. I couldn't remember. I couldn't remember whether I had put the strophanthus in with the medications. I ran into Dmitrii Georgievich's study, saw that the entire contents of his side table had been dumped on the floor, and got down on my knees to rummage through the boxes and pouches. No strophanthus. In fact, I had the distinct feeling that there hadn't been any strophanthus before, either, when I had been packing the suitcase. I ran into the bathroom. There on the shelf, above the sink, was the strophanthus. But the policeman had already gone; evidently he couldn't wait any longer. I ran to the stairs: one floor, another, a fifth; the elevator stuck between floors (as it had been for several months); finally – the door open to the street: 'Morning on the Boulevard de Courcelles,' a painting from the brush of Artist X: a line at the milk store, the sign of a florist's, a child playing with dog faeces, a departing car rounding the corner; but the pedestrians had not been drawn in yet.

As I later learned, he was put in a luxurious room in a luxurious hotel, which had been requisitioned for prominent scholars, but evidently they hadn't taken into account his age. At eighty-three it can be hard to exchange familiar surroundings, and although they assigned him a doctor, it didn't help.

Movers came for his books, and in the wink of an eye they had swept them from the shelves.

'Here's our orders,' one of them said sullenly.

Then they got to the cases in the foyer.

'Those are mine,' I said with a touch of hysteria in my voice, amazing even myself. 'Please, leave them alone.'

They left. It was strangely empty in the study now. I stopped going in there.

He died two weeks later, in his sleep.

When I called Elena Vikentievna and told her what had happened she began to wail: 'Poor, poor Nineteenth Century!'

Later the will was read. To her went the cottage near Versailles; to me all the rest. I started putting his papers in order, let the living- and dining-rooms, and got on with my life.

Much later, after the war, I learned that all three boxes of his books had been burnt somewhere due to a misunderstanding.

THREE

———◇———

TWO YEARS PASSED after the death of Dmitrii Georgievich, the war ended, and I began receiving mail from
different countries around the world on various and
sundry matters relating to his works. He was quite well
known. The University of California inquired about
purchasing his archives; a letter came from London
about reissuing his works; there was correspondence
from Norway, Holland, and Canada. I was already
accustomed to those inquiries, and it was perfectly
natural to get a letter from Stockholm, but when a
letter did arrive bearing a Swedish stamp I became
temporarily deranged. It's from Einar! At last, from
Einar! But the letter was from Olners, the Swedish
publishers. He was asking whether I wouldn't write a
biography of Dmitrii Georgievich, or, even better, a
book about him, about my life with him (*'Min lir
med . . .'*) and about his death, and wouldn't I come
to Stockholm to talk it over. In any event, the royalties
for all of Dmitrii Georgievich's works, published and
republished over the preceding eight or nine years, lay

in a bank there. The money couldn't be transferred, but I could pick it up in person. I replied that I would come as soon as I could.

My two letters to Einar came back marked 'Addressee Unknown'. That seemed odd to me. I didn't write to him any more. But I thought about him all the time. I was working at the newspaper again, and once more I was surrounded by many people, friends – close ones and mere acquaintances – and my old active, varied life, which events had disrupted, was getting back into full swing. I forgot how to wash, sew, iron, and cook, occasionally shuddered when the telephone rang, when the postman came. And with a cold, sluggish curiosity I mulled over my trip to Stockholm. It seemed to me that if he had gone to Brazil I would be able to find out about it there.

From the earliest years of my youth I had had the notion that every person has his own no man's land, a domain that is his and his alone. The life everyone sees is one thing; the other belongs to the individual, and it is none of anyone else's business. By that in no way do I mean to imply that, from an ethical standpoint, one is moral and the other amoral, or, from that of the police, one licit and the other illicit. But man lives at intervals unchecked, in freedom and in private, alone or with someone, be it for an hour a day, an evening a week, or a day a month; he lives for that private, free life of his from one evening (or day) to the next: those hours exist in a continuum.

Those hours either complement something in his

visible life or else possess some independent significance. They may be a joy or a necessity, or a habit, but they are crucial to demarcating any sort of 'general line'. If a man does not exercise this right of his, or if because of extenuating circumstances this right is denied him, he will one day wake up to find that he has never really found himself, and there is something depressing in that. I feel sorry for people who are alone only in the bathroom, never anywhere else.

An inquisition or a totalitarian state, incidentally, can never allow this second life, which eludes any and every control. It is no accident that they arrange people's lives in such a way that the only solitude permitted is that of the bathroom. Barracks and prisons often lack even that.

In this no man's land, when a man lives in freedom and private, strange things can happen: kindred souls can find each other; a book can be read and understood especially keenly, music heard in some special way. In the quiet and solitude a thought might occur that changes a man's life, ruins or saves him. Perhaps in this no man's land people cry, or drink, or think about something no one else knows, or they examine their bare feet, or they try to find a new place for a parting on their balding head, or they leaf through a picture magazine of half-naked beauties and muscle-men – I don't know, and I don't want to know. In childhood and even in adolescence (and in old age as well) we don't always feel the need for that other life. Nonetheless, it's wrong to think of that other life, that no man's land, as a luxury, and everything else as normal. That's not where the dividing line falls. It falls along the line of absolute privacy and absolute freedom.

Einar and I met in no man's land. Then something not that unusual happened: the second life flourished and came to block out the first. At the time he and I were in the stage of love that permits no thought of anything else. And we both knew what absolute privacy and absolute freedom meant. At the start of our relationship we were already talking about that, about the commandment, 'Remember the Sabbath, to keep it holy; six days shall you work, but the seventh is the Sabbath' – guard it for yourself. Each of us did have our 'Sabbath', which we jokingly called our 'Tuesday', to be funny. The 'right to Tuesday' was our favourite expression. After all, people fight for their 'Tuesday'! Let everyone be granted 'Tuesday', everyone, by decree! And laughing, we told each other, 'You're my "Tuesday",' until one day we realized that Tuesday had become the whole week.

Now, as before, my no man's land was populated by thoughts of Einar. It all came down to three questions: Is he alive? Will I ever see him again? Does he still love me? I tried not to let these thoughts undermine my foundation – my work, my relations with other people, which often were not all that straightforward, and this struggle completely sapped my emotional reserves. But inside myself, within the bounds of my second life, those hours of alarm, despair, and hope were still my private property. As always in life, I was absolute and sole master of my no man's land.

At long last the trains started running, the borders opened, arrivals and departures acquired some regularity. Through reviving, businesslike, clean Belgium, through the devastated cities of Germany – Cologne and Dusseldorf and Hamburg were to me then just like a china shop following an earthquake – through the mists of late autumn that greeted me in Denmark, with all the poetry of night-time in a sleeping car when you wake up in the pale blue light of a nightlamp and to the pleasant squeaking of something utterly homey, childlike even, as if you were flying into an abyss – but one neither homey nor childlike, in fact, a rather terrifying abyss that you will never forget and that will play a mysterious but certain role in your destiny. And the night ferry all lit up, sailing from Copenhagen to Malmö; me sitting over a glass of vermouth, nibbling on some salty crackers, gazing at the dark, the cold sea beneath me. And three Danes, who had boarded and joined me in my compartment that afternoon at Fleisburg and who took me for French, who told me that I couldn't appreciate all the splendour of the North, what with the fog, and the rain, and that I was making a mistake going to Stockholm, where at that time of year I would find only bad weather, boredom, and sullen people.

That last night I couldn't close my eyes. From time to time the conductor called out loudly in the corridor: 'Linköping! Norköping! Niuköping!' The train would stop briefly and hurry on. Patches of snow flickering outside the window beneath dark firs, villages and towns, where people were fast asleep, under the northern stars, which always shone and burned a hundred times more brightly than they ever did over Paris. A feeble northern dawn began; the air went cautiously from black to grey; the wooden houses and sheds, painted a dark red colour, under the firs, flickered their lights, issued smoke from their chimneys; and in the corridor there was movement, people were getting up, going to wash, it began to smell of coffee. A ruddy woman, smiling and curtseying, brought me a sturdy woven basket with breakfast in it, and when I opened it, on a small skillet, a fried egg still hissed, surrounded by smoked sausages that jumped in the sputtering fat as if alive.

In the half-light of morning, along the streets, lamps burned, and the trolleys, shining their pink lights, went up and down the Wasagatan, clanging their bells without stop. A taxi took me to the embankment, and to my right, across the bridge, all the stern, granite, severe beauty of Stockholm flashed before me. The water was dark grey and the sky was dark grey, and the brightly dressed children on their way to school seemed purposely scattered over the entire city in order to make it livelier, more cheerful, less grim. A token of my insanity during those moments is the agitation that seized me upon entering the Grand Hotel when a giant in galloons handed me a note: you had a phone call yesterday. A second later I was already telling myself that no one besides Olners could have known I was coming, that that stab at my heart was the purest folly, and of course, it was. Olners wished me '*Wilkommen*' and informed me that he would be at my disposal tomorrow morning at eleven.

I got out only at three o'clock, after lunch with Olners, and with the proviso that I come to his house that evening and meet his wife and sons. Leaving the publisher's, I turned on to Kungsgatan, crossed the bridge, and slowly began the descent to Melar, where on the embankment, in an enormous and evidently fairly recently completed complex that took up an entire block, Einar once lived and clearly lived no longer, since my letters never reached him. In the summer, probably, here, in the inner courtyards, they tended and mowed tiny squares of vivid grass. Now, in the quiet and vacantness, there was nothing here, a strong wind blew, the embankment was grand and severe, and on the opposite bank, in a grey autumn fog, a string of lamps burned. In the foreground, in the blackness of the November day, hung the bridge; long barges emerged from beneath it, sailing away to the Baltic, and the lights rocking on them seemed to drip on the black water, dripped and disappeared, only to reappear in the water. It smelled like a northern seacoast town, and that empire of kindred palaces, that cold silence of broad watery expanse, that embankment grandeur, the heavy sky – all of it was shot through with a Petersburg nostalgia. The north-east. Letters never reach the north-east. People never return from the north-east. Enemies came from the north-east and went back to the north-east. And I myself am now in the north-east. And my entire will is focused on not committing, not taking any kind of irrevocable step.

Entries A, B, C, and so forth. Finally I found entry K. There, to the left of the wide doorway, by the elevator, hung a directory, and as sometimes happens, before actually reading his name on it, among the other forty-odd names, I already saw that it was there. Yes, Einar still lived here, and his apartment was No. 16; but to his name on the board had been added '*och Fru*,' which means '*i Gospozha*,' which means '*et Mme*,' which means '*e Signora*,' which means 'and Mrs'. It also means '*und Frau*'. By the time I had exhausted all the languages I knew, I had to sit down on the long velvet bench that had been placed there for the convenience of those waiting for the elevator, because regardless how modern and, so to speak, 'contemporary' the building's construction, the elevator, it seemed to me, was of somewhat older build; it made the descent and ascent very slowly, and from time to time something in it clicked and even sighed. Only don't go drawing any hasty conclusions that I went anywhere in it. I simply listened to it working, sitting on the bench, while three young ladies came down in it, all dressed alike, wearing marvellous galoshes, so much the epitome of galoshes that it's a wonder they have never had their praises sung in poetry. Poets, where are your eyes? Swedish galoshes await your poems, as do their raincoats with their wonderfully cosy hoods and waterproof wonder-gloves. And don't forget the warm trousers that everyone here wears from August to June – they too await your ballades.

When I snapped out of it and stopped blithering I took a look at my watch. 4.15. It was utterly dark on the street now, it was half-raining and half-snowing, and I absolutely had to pull myself together instantly: to go to Nordisk Companiet and buy myself galoshes, gloves, a raincoat – in short, everything called for. And that is what I did. When I got back with my purchases I soaked in a hot bath for a long time, experiencing the strange feeling of absolute certainty that no one would come by, no one would call, no one would ever know what I was thinking right then or what decisions I was making.

That night I got in at about one. Besides Olners' family there had been another six guests or so, and it seemed as if each of them had invited me to his home and their names and addresses were recorded in my appointment book. This was gracious Sweden, which wanted nothing but to entertain me, to feed me, to be nice to me and to give me gifts.

I never did have to decide anything, though. Accustomed to living in a big city, to living – when I so desired – totally anonymously, I never dreamed what a small town Stockholm was. I couldn't have known that in it there were all of two or three acceptable bourgeois places to dine or spend an evening, that if you stayed for a week you might even start seeing a familiar face or two, and that it was quite common to observe friends running into each other on the street, which happens so rarely in Paris. I wound up my affairs in a week, in seven days, or rather, seven evenings, having been in seven different homes, at seven different parties, where, however, I always met the same people. I picked up a large (by my lights) sum of money and even got permission to take it out of the country. That last evening I went to see *Rigoletto* with the entire Olners family – wife, sons, daughters-in-law, and grandson – and was dressed head to toe in new, newly purchased clothes: linen, stockings, shoes, dress, even a fur coat. After the performance a gang of us proceeded rather noisily to the restaurant right there in the Opera House, huge, half-dark, and comfortable, where among other elegant and equally noisy people we were seated at a long table. When we had all taken our seats and before the head waiter had brought our menus, I not only saw Einar sitting quite nearby but his eyes and mine met altogether naturally. Not taking his eyes from my face, he started to stand, slowly, holding his napkin in his hand, his mouth spread in an artificial, unpleasant smile that was utterly new to me. Then he dropped the napkin on his chair and walked towards me, and I saw that he had got himself under control. His somewhat older face expressed precisely what he wanted it to: pleasant surprise at running into an old friend. His face went back to its old self.

Conversation at his table stopped, and at that

moment I had the sensation of quiet suddenly descending all around me as well. In that silence it was as if I were observing myself, something that happens to me very rarely and that I don't like. It usually lasts a few seconds, but the feeling can be torturous: here I sit wearing a new dress, my new handbag is lying by my place; the hairdresser has cut my black hair short and combed it back, revealing my forehead and ears; I'm wearing a new perfume, I can smell it; my left hand is resting on the tablecloth, my right is touching my glass, I see a ring with a topaz. Now she's going to smile and speak, I think about myself, and I make an effort to put an end to this being divided in two. It passes by itself.

A very plump, huge lady and a man at Einar's table turned toward me. I got a better look at her when we both stood up and, meeting half-way between tables, exchanged oddly casual, jubilant greetings. The exclamations began: Olners knew Einar quite well but hadn't seen him for a long time (i.e., two months or so, apparently). After a brief disarray, while everyone was scurrying about, shuffling chairs and rearranging tables, they all took their seats, smiling and shaking hands. Broken French began to flow all around, and glasses were raised – to me, to Russia, to France, to my forthcoming book about Dmitrii Georgievich, whom Olners compared with Mendeleev in a short but very cleverly improvised speech.

Einar's wife was a blue-eyed giantess with light brown hair, a round doll's face, big round cheeks that puffed out a little, bringing to mind a chubby angel or, if you prefer, an angel blowing a trumpet. Rubens and Bellini all in one. She moved sedately, as befits a woman who is bigger not only than all the other women but also than many of the men in the room. She gave me a quick once-over and then, without the slightest trace of self-consciousness, said loudly: 'Einar, why did you tell me Olga looked like a Chinawoman? There's nothing the least bit Chinese about her!'

I did not leave the next day. I left only four days later. I spent four evenings with them, and in the afternoon Emma and I strolled about town, took a daytrip to Skansen, visited Strindberg's grave and saw the enormous wooden cross with the gold inscription. One late afternoon we even wandered over to the Tivoli, where we shot at targets, played billiards and looked at freaks. She admitted to me that she had sent both my letters back because she didn't want Einar, who was so happy with her and for whom all emotional strife had ceased ever since he'd met her, to renew a correspondence with me. They had both tried to arrange their life amicably, in peace and love. 'We accept the autumn as well as the spring,' as Emma put it, 'like everything in nature, and we both love good weather and a rainbow in the sky.' They had been married five years already, 'and don't think,' she said, holding a pastry in her hand, 'that we've become so bogged down in our sensible domestic bliss that we never think about our old friends. I myself have very close friends in Italy, dear people, friends of my innocent youth,' (she wasn't joking) 'and through all these years of war both Einar and I have been so worried, so distressed . . . especially the hardships, and when the bombings . . . You see we always had everything here. Naturally no grapes were shipped here in the spring, but is that so important? Tell me, I want to know, do you care whether or not there are grapes in spring?'

In the evenings I went to their place and we all sat together – Emma, Einar, Dr Mattis, and I – in an overheated room, in low-slung chairs. I talked more than anyone else: about those years, about Dmitrii Georgievich and the cold hearth he so often sat in front of towards the end – whereas here the hearth burned with thick birch logs so dry that they caught from a single match – about the four visits, about the mistakenly burned books, about our reading aloud in the evenings by candlelight, about the fact that there wasn't enough fuel and how very cold it could get in winter, about the key role wool and lard play in human life. Then I would think, suddenly, that I needn't go into such detail. Better to tell them about Dr Wengland and their conversation in Dmitrii Georgievich's study behind closed doors. Did he or did he not inform? That remained a mystery to me.

'Of course he did,' said Emma firmly.

Dr Mattis said, 'Maybe he slipped unintentionally.'

But Einar just kept smoking. And so I talked and talked, and they listened, and I told them about the strophanthus and said that Dmitrii Georgievich might have lived longer, perhaps to a natural end, if I had put the strophanthus in the suitcase then.

'Under no circumstances!' said Emma.

'Very doubtful,' said Dr Mattis.

We dined late on cold chicken and white wine, and fresh strawberries, which at that time of year were still more of a rarity than grapes in spring. And all this was possible only because there, by the elevator, my first day in Stockholm, I had decided never to see Einar again.

In all those four days she never left Einar and me alone together. Nor was there any phone call from him. And if, despite my decision, I was waiting for her permission, I never got it. All three of them came to see me off at the station, and Emma and I strolled up and down the platform while Dr Mattis and Einar went through the cars in search of some Gustafson who they thought was planning to make the trip to Antwerp that day. While Emma and I walked, we talked about how perhaps, in a year, we might go to Italy, stay a while in Florence, Venice – in two years at the very most. She looked at me intently, as if she were sizing me up, turning something over in her mind, and she told me that she liked me 'awfully' well, that she hadn't expected me to be so sweet, so cheerful, and more things like that, and I had the feeling that everything was happening and would happen in the future just as she decided. Later we laughed at some mistake of hers in French, and she taught me how to protest in Swedish if the conductor kept me awake again at night with his cries of 'Linköping! Norköping! Niuköping!' They failed to locate Gustafson. I stood on the steps and shook hands with all three of them, and just before the train pulled out a messenger suddenly appeared with a bouquet of white lilac from Olners – white lilac in November, more precious than strawberries or grapes in spring.

And so a woman I scarcely knew, with the face of a cherub, smiling and entertaining me, would not let Einar be alone with me for a minute, would not let him call me (I suspected he did not go to his office all that time). Without the slightest embarrassment she had informed me that she had sent both my letters back, invited me into her home, talked Einar and Dr Mattis into coming to the train station – and the end results were utterly the same as if she had locked her Einar up, or incarcerated me in the cellar of the Gestapo, or under lock and key in a luxurious hotel room. All the while I was running around to museums, stores, and other people's living-rooms, I was in her custody. Amid all the melancholic, autumnal beauty of black Melar, in the fires of the Petersburg nostalgia of her 'half-Chinawoman, half-Frenchwoman' (as she laughingly referred to me), here I had no more no man's land than Dmitrii Georgievich had had in the Majestic or the Bristol or wherever; only I hadn't died, as he had, because I was twice as young and fed on wild strawberries, sturgeon and grouse, all washed down with punch.

But in that hot night train I could feel myself now

going from impotent rage to cruel insult at Einar for not having done anything to spend so much as an hour with me somewhere, freely and privately, to make me his 'Tuesday' once again for just one time. Was there really anything at all to explain to me? Wasn't everything quite clear as it was? He had waited two years, the war had dragged on, he had married, built himself a life (Yesterday she had said: 'I had to move in with him; it's been years since anyone has been able to find an apartment here at any price, and so here we are, living on top of one another, with part of the furniture in storage'); he had married, and now, with Emma, he could 'accept the autumn as well as the spring'.

No, there was nothing to explain, and no point in belabouring the past, but maybe we could have spent a little time together? And suddenly I pictured what that would have been like and realized that that didn't matter to him at all. It mattered only to me, so that I could say to him: 'You know, Einar, my friend, Emma really has you under her thumb. Why, she doesn't give you your mail!' And at that moment, in powerless and bitter despair, I felt as if I were burning up with hatred, grief, and outrage. In the corridor the conductor was calling out, and we were stopping somewhere.

Despite everything I still loved him, and only him, and no matter how many times I repeated to myself that he didn't want anything to do with me, that didn't make me love him any less. Maybe I loved him all the more seeing him in Stockholm. My whole life was filled with my hopeless love for him, which prevented me from settling my own fate, and put a terrible burden on all my days and nights, a burden from which I could not, or perhaps would not, disembarrass myself.

FOUR

———◇———

RETURNING HOME, I immediately plunged into postwar work life, which I felt it necessary to go about sensibly. Above all, I resolved to get rid of the old apartment on the Boulevard de Courcelles, a perfectly reasonable place for Dmitrii Georgievich to live before the 'other' war but no good for me at all. I exchanged that enormous, dark, old, Russian residence for a small, sunny apartment on the Left Bank and, with the aid of Elena Vikentievna, sorted through his old Russian things.

The apartment had been taken even before the 'other' war ('in the era of electric filters and the wave method,' as Olners put it), and it was here that Dmitrii Georgievich's wife and my mother had brought various items from Petersburg.

'This is all archeology!' said Elena Vikentievna, who had sold her cottage in Versailles, had opened her own millinery studio, and was planning to get married. 'Sediment from entire eras! Pounds of Russian silver! Signed works by Korovin! A present from Chichibabin

– a marble boy removing the famous splinter from his heel. Ipatiev had completely different taste: a silver pail engraved with some sort of dates . . . People really knew how to live! A sketch of Fontainebleau by Benois. That's from after the "other" war, but before this one.'

'He used to visit us. I remember him.'

'And who didn't visit you! I can imagine! An embroidered cushion . . .'

'That's a present from Mechnikov's widow, from about twenty years ago. For his birthday.'

'Look at this: what a bunch! Two dozen old biddies!'

'That's "Graduation, 1908".'

'Saints alive!'

The letters and manuscripts she wouldn't touch. She watched anxiously as I packed them away in boxes, but the books on the shelves, in the foyer, she did help me sort. Here there were many with inscriptions – books by his contemporaries, born, as was he, in the sixties, as well as the fifties, of the previous century. Many of those inscribers I had known. Some had died only recently; others just before this war. Not one was still alive. A. A. Plescheev – who later went blind and walked in tatters with a white cane, he who as a child had seen Dostoevsky – inside his *Reminiscences* had written 'To the Sun of our science!' followed by a long blot. Elena Vikentievna even shed a few tears.

'I remember him walking around town,' she said with a sigh, 'stopping at corners and saying, "*Aidez-moi à traverser,*" and how one time someone gave him alms . . . The Sun of our science!'

Things started going smoothly and well once I
decided to give over one of my future apartment's
three rooms wholly to Dmitrii Georgievich's past.
Hardest of all was dealing with two immense paintings
of unknown authorship: 'The Governor Receiving
Visitors' and 'The Funeral of a Second Guild Mer-
chant'. In the end – without regrets – I had a dealer
take them, but something still bothered me, so I
begged Elena Vikentievna to take an embroidered
pillow – a copy of the Sistine Madonna in satin stitch –
and a tiny vase, and the boy removing the thorn from
his foot. The dealer's cart on the street downstairs, and
on it the 'antiquarian' (as he dignified himself) loaded
threadbare rugs, worn out armchairs, jangling chan-
deliers, tasselled drapes, a bronze desk set, copper pots
which as far as I could remember had never been used.
Then Elena Vikentievna took two baskets home in a
taxi, and at twilight the movers arrived, bringing
whatever else there was that could be of use to me in
the twentieth century. In my new place, in the
evenings, when I got back from the newspaper, I sorted
and packed away everything that was later to go to the
University of California. And since my new place had
no fireplace, no real stove, one evening I had to take all
twenty-two neatly bound packets of letters (most of
them from family) to the place of friends whose old
house had a stove, and we spent hours burning them in
it, pensively stirring the smouldering, flyaway ashes
with the poker.
After that, life took off. Only my no man's land

remained the same as before: thoughts about Einar, thoughts about the distant and not-so-distant past, thoughts about Emma, about Stockholm, about my future, which seemed to be impossible without him and improbable with him.

Occasionally Emma wrote to me. Her letters were a mixture of French and German and dealt chiefly with the seasons: We have a lot of snow, the children made a snowman in our yard – a nice custom, don't you think? The days are getting longer – that gives everyone energy and courage; winter is not forever, we tell ourselves. Soon it will be Easter, we wish you a happy holiday! The warm days have begun and we are going to the skerries for a month – it will be marvellous to get away from the bustle of the city, to live surrounded by nature in the company of one's own thoughts; it can be so helpful to think something through well, as I'm certain you too appreciate. If you were here, the white nights would remind you of your childhood, but you would have to get used to them. They have a bad effect on some people. Dr Mattis is with us. We go swimming and boating and spend our time very enjoyably. Einar says he's a little bored, but I don't believe him. He looks wonderful and got himself a big dog, a Great Dane, a pedigree – don't you think there's something ennobling about animals? Today we lit a fire, we've already had a frost. We've had five days of fog in the city, I'm sitting at home with a cold. What's good about being sick is that suddenly you find the time to read a good book . . . Merry Christmas! We all three wish you a happy New Year! We hope to see you in the coming year! And then again: We wish you a happy Easter! We are thinking about going to Italy this summer. And then a month later: We've decided to spend a month in Venice. Take some time off and come visit us. And a letter from the beginning of July: We've taken an apartment near San Zaccaria, there's a room for you.

I sat down at my desk, took out a sheet of paper, a pen, and feeling myself a liar with every word, wrote:

Dear Emma and Einar!
    Thank you for your invitation. I'd be happy to see you both and spend a week with you. I'm taking time off and will be there on the 15th; I believe the train arrives in the evening. If Dr Mattis is with you, send him my greetings.
Yours, Olga

That's what I wrote, 'Yours, Olga' without even thinking. In general those days I was doing my best not to think: if I started to think then I certainly would do the sensible thing and stay in Paris and punish myself for it afterwards. This was fate in its old-fashioned carriage graciously lowering the steps to me and inviting me to sit down, and if I were to think and think seriously I would think myself into a nasty predicament: fate was simply giving me a hand up so that it could topple me over, throw me down, and fall on top of me . . . I even told myself sometimes:

Haven't I done too much thinking in my lifetime? Other people don't think and they live happily enough. Come on, for once in your life let yourself not think. Take the invitation at face value, don't let's probe too deeply, into what its real purpose is, let's accept Venice as one would a present – not as if every box of candy or bouquet of flowers inevitably had a snake wriggling or a bat flying out of it.

I had only one childhood memory of Venice, that was before the 'other' war and I was five years old. By the way, that perhaps sole memory from childhood has to do directly with Dmitrii Georgievich. True, as a child I was always hearing, Dmitrii Georgievich has come, Dmitrii Georgievich is working, Dmitrii Georgievich went out on business, but I never had anything to do with him directly. Whereas I do recall one evening in Venice. On a small balcony, probably not very high up, but to me it seemed as if we were sitting in a high tower, two chairs had been put out. I sat on one of them, and on the other, wearing a tussore jacket and a Panama hat, sat Dmitrii Georgievich, a fat book in hand. Probably it was the hotel on the Lido where we had found ourselves then: his wife, my mother, and I. Probably it was an exceptional night for me to have been left with him because I don't remember that ever happening again. My mouth and my eyes opened wide, I listened to him read me Pushkin's 'Ruslan and Ludmila' aloud. Probably he had decided it was time I made my acquaintance with Russian literature.

'I shall read you' – that is approximately how he began his preface – 'a brilliant composition by a brilliant Russian poet. "By Lukomorye a green oak stands." One day you'll understand, so to speak, the full power of that expression: Lukomorye! Sea's Bend! Here we are by the sea, passing the time, so to speak, a summer's holiday, but that's still not Lukomorye.' He was forever getting flustered with me over his formal and informal 'you's.' '"A golden chain hangs from that oak." In its time the line aroused a great deal of debate, because here we have two theories as to the possible provenance, so to speak, of that chain. The Druids, as you know, mmm, lived under the oaks. But there is also a cat here, which, on the one hand, is the cat of folklore, of olden times, about which the late Alexander Nikolaevich related so many interesting facts to me in his time, and on the other hand this is a symbolic cat. Let us continue: "And day and night along the chain this learned cat circles round and round."'

The rest followed without commentary, but for that reason very little of it registered with me. The learned cat stuck in my memory and an entire picture became engraved there approximately as follows: in a high tower, by some sort of Lukomorye, Dmitrii Georgievich and I are sitting, my mouth can't seem to stay shut and inside it's all dried out from rapturous amazement and reverence, since Dmitrii Georgievich has passed on a bit of news: a certain learned cat has lived in Venice since ancient times. Not only that, evidently he is quite well known to Dmitrii Georgievich.

Other than that I didn't remember anything about Venice, and when the vaporetto took me from the station down the Grand Canal and the time-blackened stone lace of palaces opened up to my right and to my left, I felt as if I'd been hurled into another dimension, where everything all around had become light, lacy, airy, where one could never (and would never want to) measure life and oneself in it by the old standards, where all around had suddenly become different, the impossible possible, the difficult easy, the hopeless sad and happy at the same time. Here and there between buildings narrow canals opened out, minuscule bridges across them, churches dissolving in the dusk; pale pink in the pink air, lights shone stock-still or appeared to flutter above the water; utterly otherworldly, magical, starrily green colours from the lights criss-crossed them. A sensation of eerie, underwater slow motion filled me throughout, the feeling of a special, slowed rhythm hitherto unknown to me, in which my breathing, all my movements, fused with the movement of the vaporetto, where the decrepitude and impoverishment of the palaces, which watched the water and me in their inscrutable charm and pensiveness, swam by, their mournful immobility palpable.

When to my left, still inside that astounding rhythm of criss-crossing lights and shadows, the broad embankment with the Doges' Palace appeared and, to the right, the lagoon, laden with some unknowable nocturnal significance, I felt an onrush of almost unendurable happiness at the thought that in a few

minutes I would see Einar and he would be with me in
this bewitching, twilit world. When the vaporetto
docked, I was drawn to the exit. A boy porter grabbed
my suitcase in one hand and put the other on his
shoulder and directed me to go ahead. I stepped
ashore. Emma opened her arms wide, Dr Mattis was
standing next to her.

'This is Mario,' she said, presenting someone to me. I
looked, Einar was standing behind her shoulder. 'Oh,
how good you've arrived!' she exclaimed. 'Oh, how
wonderful this is all going to be! Einar, give her a kiss.
You're so terribly happy to see her! And we haven't
seen each other for so long!'

He dutifully leaned over and kissed me on the cheek.
It happened so quickly that I didn't manage to say
anything or to make any private gesture. Dr Mattis
stood watching us both. He seemed out of sorts.

One large room of the apartment let out on to a quiet
square with a church; the master bedroom for Emma
and Einar gave out over a toy-sized garden behind the
house. Dr Mattis, the servant, and I had tiny rooms
along the hallway which looked out on to an inner
courtyard where a small fountain gurgled and some
woman washed laundry day and night. Steps led from
one room to another; apparently part of the apartment
was an old stone house, and another part had been
added on later. In the main room, where we had
supper and then sat for a long time, there was the same
calm order and stolid northern comfort of a well-lived-
in place that Emma, evidently, carried around with

her wherever she went. But what was new was the presence of Mario, whom Emma told me was an old friend from her youth, that she had known him before the war in Florence, where she had at one time studied painting; that was before this war, and now he had come to Venice to meet and reminisce. 'He already has four children,' Emma cried. 'Mario, show her the photographs!'

Later Mario left and Einar (who smoked a pipe now, which gave him an excuse to speak even less) began to question me – very thoroughly, as becomes a gracious host – about my life, my new apartment, my new friends, my work. Emma listened, but she had a distracted look about her. Dr Mattis, who was planning to leave early the following day on an outing, finally went to his room, and soon after that I said good-night as well. Alone in my room, where I could hear the fountain's gurgling. I turned on the light, looked around, saw my things, my half-emptied suitcase, the white walls, the mat on the floor, the muslin on the window, the sweet, simple objects on the dresser: an ashtray, an oddly shaped bottle, a brightly coloured cloth, a tumbler of rainbow glass. Tomorrow. What was going to happen tomorrow? I sat down on the bed and, taking one more look around, told myself that I had come here in the hope of getting to be alone with Einar finally, of telling him that I had written, of asking him if he loved me, of making him tell me how it had all come about; I came here to tell him I still loved him as ever, that I couldn't go on living like this any more, without any word from him. Did he really just up and brush me aside, push me out of his life, without a single word? And now? Why had they wanted me to come? Or did he always want the same thing as Emma?

It was after nine when I woke up and listened closely to the strange sounds: the light clatter of dishes, a woman's song – probably the servant singing – steps back and forth along the hall; the fountain gurgling, the bucket rattling; a pigeon cooing somewhere very close by. I jumped up, got washed and dressed, and went out to the dining-room.

'I was just waiting for you,' said Einar from the armchair by the window, an English paper in his hands. 'Let's have some coffee.'

We sat down across from each other and a Swedish breakfast appeared on the table, everything there was supposed to be, without which Einar could not live even in Paris. But wait, just wait, I told myself, suddenly happening on a completely new thought. Was it really necessary that he rush straightaway out of France then, on 2 September of that terrible year? Was it really imperative that he dash off home to his father (who looked like King Gustaf), his Russian nanny, his brother who was getting ready to go to Brazil, to peaceful Sweden, away from cannon-thundered Europe, no matter what, as fast as his legs could carry him? Was it really that none of the 'neutrals' remained among us then? Was there really a law requiring everyone to go back to where he came from?

No, there wasn't any such law, I think. That came much later. I remember very well a Swiss I knew who never went anywhere. I ran into him at Christmas, that was in '39, maybe even in '40. There was also the family of an American lawyer that continued to live on our staircase, something that had never occurred to me before. That family stayed until the fall of 1941, when, finally, they left. Much later seals were placed on the doors.

'Now we're going to go for a walk and I'm going to show you everything, everything, everything,' said Einar. 'I'm going to take you all around until this evening.'

'Where's Emma?'

'Emma went away to Torcello with Dr Mattis.'

'Went away! For the whole day? Was she planning to?'

'She got ready in a minute, and they took Mario with them.'

I felt like some sort of a trap had been set for me, set from the very beginning, the very day she'd written: 'We've taken an apartment, there's a room for you.' No, much earlier, in Stockholm, at the train station, when she'd said, I think: 'Why don't you come stay with us for a time in Italy when we're there?'

Einar and I went out and started off at a leisurely pace up the Riva degli Schiavoni to the square. Through the tension I experienced that day I was constantly aware of his total tranquillity, his inner freedom, his conviction that everything he was doing

was right. I must confess that I, rather than resisting
him, in an hour or two felt much calmer and freer. We
even had a few good laughs together. After lunch,
when we were sitting at Florian's, he asked quite
simply whether there weren't any Russian poems that
had something to say about this.

'About what?' I asked, and I experienced an inward
fright that there was going to be something like an
explanation.

'Why, about Venice,' he said.

'There are a lot, quite a lot,' I replied. 'One day, not
right now, I'll recite them all to you.'

'I knew it,' he said very pleased, smiling happily.

Towards evening Emma came home alone.

'We never went to Torcello,' she said nonchalantly.
'When we got to the pier there was no room, and Dr
Mattis had to go alone, so Mario and I went to the
Lido, had a swim and lunch. I've got a terrible burn.'
She lowered her dress from her shoulder; her upper arm
was flaming red.

Einar went out somewhere, and Emma and I sat
down by the table and drank coffee. She was in high
spirits, she talked a lot, she took her temperature (she
loved to take her temperature daily) and assured me
that if she did have a fever then it was due to sunburn.
But she didn't.

The next morning Emma and Mario went to
Torcello ('I always get what I want,' was her remark),
and once again Einar and I were left to ourselves.

That day and the three succeeding days I remember

now with mixed feelings: they held the expectation of something, something I wanted with such a passion, the something I'd come here for, as well as an uncomfortable, practically scary presentiment that the very thing I was hoping for was precisely what ought never to come about, that I could never accept it, that it was sort of like alms proffered to suit the giver, and proffered not to me alone but to Einar and me both. Added to this was the impression everything I'd seen had made on me: the colourful crowd on the Piazza San Marco, the constant celebration of lights and shadows; the dusk of the Scuola San Rocco, the hundreds of paintings I'd seen – gaping clouds with the Almighty, the slippers of Carpaccio's Ursula, and Bellini's trumpeting angels, so familiar to me. Einar was with me, we wandered through the halls of the Accademia, talked sometimes but sometimes not, walked out on to hunchback little bridges, sat on squares, sometimes nameless squares, on the steps of the Frati Church, wandered some more, and by then I was certain that this was all Emma's doing, she had set it all up: both the coming of red-faced, broad-shouldered Mario and me.

On the fifth day of my stay Dr Mattis left. He looked disgruntled, and he had begun addressing us all quite brusquely, almost rudely.

'He's been having an unhappy romance with an English girl,' Emma said derisively. 'It seems she left for Rome yesterday.'

But I didn't believe her. His departure put me in a

distressing and at the same time rather absurd posi-
tion: I didn't want the three of us to be left alone.

'You don't realize how we feel about you,' Emma
said to me that evening, as if she had guessed that I was
planning to move up my departure. 'In these past few
days you've become one of us, and Einar has such a
good time being with you. And I am so terribly fond of
you.'

She loved the word 'terribly', whereas I didn't at all.
Did I believe her? No, not for a moment, but believing
her would have been very hard, whereas not believing
her would have been even harder. It was clear to me
now: she had been schooling me since the first moment
of my arrival. The learned cat lived in Venice, I
recalled, and I had no desire to be anything like him.

I could not allow her to lay hands on my fate, to
grant or not grant me entry into any portion of my
universe, to my own private no man's land according
to her convenience. She was going to the theatre, La
Fenice, with Mario that evening, and she told us
offhandedly, feigning distraction, that there was to be
a full moon today and we could take a ride over to San
Giorgio Maggiore. If I were to listen to her, then, with
her permission, I would surely be less unhappy, but I
could not obey her; somehow or other I had to decide
everything myself, and go away from here. She was
showing me the way, but I would follow another path.
I am my own person, private and free, and I am and
will be my own master, and when it comes to that I
will not tolerate her interference.

I had been sitting at Florian's watching the strolling crowds for a long time. As I had once before, gazing at dark, wartime Paris, I thought: How much suffering there has been here, so much passion, the world's and Russians'; there is even a drop here of my own smallest and greatest suffering. Einar came up to my table. His face was happy, he had a tan, he had slimmed down, and, looking younger, he reminded me of the old Einar.

'Let's go to San Giorgio Maggiore,' he said. 'We have at least two hours of freedom while they're at the theatre.' Those words struck me, hurt me, shook me.

'Two hours of freedom,' I echoed. 'Freedom for what?'

He sat down and, before ordering anything, greedily drank the rest of the lemon and ice from my glass.

'I'm so thirsty,' he said. 'I've been wanting to ask you, why didn't you ever write to me?'

'What can I say?' I said. 'I don't know myself. Time passed, everything changed. It wasn't easy to write. Actually, I did write to you, but I never sent the letters.'

He looked at me, intent. He hadn't looked at me like that in a long time.

'Why are you looking at me like that, Einar? Don't you know whether it's all right or not? Of course it is, since you're allowed.'

'I don't understand what you're talking about.'

But I didn't answer, and he, evidently, could tell by my face that I wasn't going to San Giorgio Maggiore. Cautiously he took my hand and held it in his own warm, large hands. An orchestra was playing somewhere, the celebrating continued all around us, people were walking about here who were cheerful, but I was not cheerful, and . . . 'the thinking reed grumbled its revolt.'

'You know, Einar,' I said, not taking my hand away from him, 'when I was a young girl I once had a terrible disappointment (this is me telling you about Russian poetry) when I found out that our great romantic poet Tyuchev helped himself to a line of a French philosopher! The Frenchman called a human being a "thinking reed", and the Russian thought a man a reed in revolt. Actually, to this day I've never recovered from it!'

He laughed, and I laughed, and ever so gently I took my hand away and moved my chair closer to him:

'I'm leaving tomorrow, Einar.' I looked at him closely, and especially into his eyes. 'I want to tell you in parting that I've learned a thing or two over the years. Now when a door cracks open or a gate lifts slightly I'm not going to be suffocated by tears of gratitude any more, no, I'm not! I'm not going to jump at every possibility or bow to just anyone's permission. After all I've seen I have no wish to be, even in the littlest thing, that grey cattle that they mobilize, drill, march off somewhere, stuff with ice-cream sundaes or starve, punish or make walk the plank.'

'No one's punishing you or stuffing you with ice-cream sundaes.'

'I want to tell you something else: if you allow anyone to arrange your no man's land, then in the end, reasoning logically, it will reach the point where they put you in a luxurious suite of a luxurious hotel and burn your books and drive away everyone you ever loved. Give in just a little and there's no limit to how far they'll go. They'll take away everything. Where does it end, Einar? Where is privacy and freedom? Two policemen (Mario reminded me of one of them actually!), an investigator, a judge – everyone's going to take a piece of your turf.'

Now he understood, I could tell by his eyes. He understood it all, through and through. I knew him too well. He even understood that I had written to him, that I loved him. And that his complacent happiness at being allowed to do everything had shaken me. One minute passed, then another, but he didn't say anything in reply. Not that I was expecting one: I hadn't asked him any questions.

We had gone back and I was beginning to pack my things, and he was sitting silently on the windowsill. I set my alarm for 7.30 so as not to be late for the train the next morning.

When they got back from the theatre, Emma was shocked.

'You're home? Didn't you go anywhere?'

'No,' I said. 'It didn't work out somehow. We sat at Florian's, and then I packed.'

The four of us went into the dining-room and while we were having our first course I noticed Mario and Emma looking at me with poorly concealed distaste. I also noticed that sparks were flying between the two of them. When she handed him his glass he put his hand on her fingers.

Meanwhile Einar was saying: 'They cleaned off the top layer, removed the paint, and underneath found Saint Sebastian. Who could have imagined such a story!'

'As soon as they get sick of each other, or his wife demands Mario's return, Emma will drive me away triumphantly,' I thought, and I drained my glass. 'I'm not about to give her that satisfaction.'

I left them, saying I wanted to get to bed early. Thank you for everything. Maybe we'll see each other again sometime in Paris – not this year, surely, or the next, but maybe in two? Emma hugged me, we kissed each other noisily on both cheeks.

'Goodbye, Mario, goodbye, Einar,' I said.

In the morning the vaporetto took me past the palaces, through the green water of the Grand Canal, to the station; I barely made it to the train, and the porter crammed me into my car. A peculiarity of Venice: vanishing instantaneously, not running after the train, not nodding first to the left and then to the right, as other cities do when you leave them, but swallowed up in an instant, as if it had never been.